"Patricia MacDo...
apparent to Mary...
of female-...
—*The Plai...*

Praise for #1 international bestselling author
Patricia MacDonald and

MARRIED TO A STRANGER

"Fans of Mary Higgins Clark and Nancy Taylor Rosenberg will find *Married to a Stranger* a mesmerizing reading experience. . . . As with Hitchcock's terrific *Suspicion*, readers will wonder until the very end whether David wants his wife dead. Patricia MacDonald is one of the top suspense writers of the past few years."

—*Midwest Book Review*

"Long on expertly frayed nerves."

—*Kirkus Reviews*

"Recommended reading for Mary Higgins Clark fans and others who like their mysteries fast paced and told from the female point of view."

—*Booklist*

**A Featured Alternate Selection of the
Doubleday Book Club, The Literary Guild,
and The Mystery Guild**

Married to a Stranger is also available as an
eBook

NO WAY HOME

THE GIRL NEXT DOOR

"Absolutely intriguing! I couldn't put the book down."

—Lisa Jackson, *New York Times* bestselling author

"Another sure winner . . . [from] the master of small-town tragedy."

—*Booklist*

"The suspense builds with each chapter. . . . A dark tale with an unexpected twist."

—*The Orlando Sentinel* (FL)

"Gripping. . . . I read it start to finish in one sitting."

—Carla Neggers, *New York Times* bestselling author

"Fans of Mary Higgins Clark will want to read *The Girl Next Door*."

—*Midwest Book Review*

"Compelling suspense . . . enthralling."

—*Romantic Times* (Top Pick)

"Patricia MacDonald tells a good story."

—*The Charlotte Observer* (NC)

Her Edgar Award nominee!
THE UNFORGIVEN

"A creepy page-turner that stays in your head and haunts you for days. . . . A gripping read from page one."

—curledup.com

MARRIED
TO A
Stranger

PATRICIA
MacDONALD

POCKET BOOKS
New York London Toronto Sydney

POCKET BOOKS, a division of Simon & Schuster, Inc.
1230 Avenue of the Americas, New York, NY 10020

This book is a work of fiction. Names, characters, places and incidents are products of the author's imagination or are used fictitiously. Any resemblance to actual events or locales or persons, living or dead, is entirely coincidental.

Originally published in hardcover in 2006 by Atria Books

ISBN-13: 978-0-7432-6959-9
ISBN-10:   0-7432-6959-4

This Pocket Books paperback edition July 2007

10 9 8 7 6 5 4 3 2 1

POCKET and colophon are registered trademarks
of Simon & Schuster, Inc.

Cover design by Jae Song

Manufactured in the United States of America

For information regarding special discounts for bulk purchases, please contact Simon & Schuster Special Sales at 1-800-456-6798 or business@simonandschuster.com.

To my friend Mary Jane Salk,
who is glamorous and witty, wise and good

ACKNOWLEDGMENTS

Special thanks to Dr. Jacqueline Moyerman for insights, information, and ever-interesting discussions. And thanks, as always, to the team who kept me on the blacktop through this detour-filled trip: Art Bourgeau, Sara Bourgeau, Meg Ruley, Jane Berkey, and Maggie Crawford.

Thanks also to Louise Burke, for the beautiful paperbacks, to Peggy Gordjin for taking me to many foreign ports, and to all at Albin Michel in Paris, especially Tony Cartano, Francis Esminard, Joelle Faure, Danielle Boespflug, Sandrine Labrevois, and Florence Godfernaux for innumerable kindnesses.

MARRIED
TO A
Stranger